To a Very good fri...d
Flore

Wyora &
Mildred

The Windwalker

The Windwalker

Blaine M. Yorgason

Bookcraft
Salt Lake City, Utah

Library of Congress Catalog Card Number: 78-75366
ISBN 0-88494-362-3

First Edition

6th Printing, 1981

Lithographed in the United States of America
PUBLISHERS PRESS
Salt Lake City, Utah

To Melvin Luke, an old friend who first
showed me the value of age; to John K.
Child, a very special friend; and to Frank C.
McCarthy, whose painting "The Lookout"
gave me the inspiration for the cover
art and, ultimately, for this story.

Aging

Time? we asked.
A strange word, that,
with meaning none too clear.
That's right, God said.
Here time is not,
but soon will be—
down there.

Time is a minute,
an hour, a day,
a week, a month,
a year.
Time is part of eternity,
frozen—
and always there.

For earth, you see
is a school of sorts,
where you will go to learn.
And you remain only
a little time
before you must
return.

But how will we know,
someone then asked,
just how much time we have?
And how can we tell
when school is through,
and we return to you,
at last?

Good questions, those,
Heavenly Father replied,
and I will tell you here.
I'll give you age

that you may know
when time has passed
down there.

A baby you'll start
with body new—
and time for you begins.
Through childhood, youth,
and then adult,
I'll give you weeks
and years.

And as your schooling
nears its end,
it's time for you to leave,
I'll give you wrinkles,
aches and pains,
and other
infirmities.

Thus you will know full well,
dear ones,
that your time on earth is through.
For age will be
your counting-clock.
Aging—my gift
to you.

Blaine M. Yorgason

Contents

Foreword

There are those who look at the aged with eyes of impatience, merely tolerating if not inwardly resenting their daily intrusion. After all, they say, with the demands of today, why be burdened and bothered? In *The Windwalker*, we find not only justification for, but great wisdom in sitting at the feet of those who have entered the autumn of their lives.

In this book, the author has ladled freely from the well of life's lessons. This is accomplished through the eyes of a people who, perhaps more than any others, have accepted aging as the common denominator of life, and have faced it squarely. The American Indian and his ancestors had an advanced culture and a deeply religious nature long before the white man made his appearance. In fact, when the first Europeans encountered the native Americans, they were astounded at how close their beliefs were to Christianity. This is why the author chose to look at aging, faith, and teaching from the earthy yet spiritual viewpoint of the Indian.

As his brother, it has been my privilege to observe the author feel his way from the inception of this book to its completed form. For many years the author has studied and researched the lives of the native Americans, gaining great respect for their culture and beliefs. He has also, over the past several years, become deeply involved with many of those we arbitrarily label as aged, learning from them as he has watched them struggle to recognize and accept themselves as elderly yet still valuable citizens. Even so, the author's insights and understanding extend past the color of a man and the wrinkles in his skin, to life itself. This you will also come to know as you enjoy reading and gleaning from the pages that follow.

BRENTON G. YORGASON

Introduction

As Indians, we are moved when we contemplate the Windwalker, an old man who is a child of Mother Earth and the Great Creator. Through him we see the spirit of our people, a people with total reverence for life — reverence for Earthmaker, the Giver-of-life; for our relationship with Him; for the earth, which is seen not as an object for exploitation but as an inseparable part of existence and a complement in forming eternity.

Our people believe that Giver-of-life created the Mother Earth, water, plants, mountains, rocks, man, and all elements in this world. By respectfully acknowledging that each creation has a spirit and an intellect and thus is brother to all others, we express respect and reverence to Giver-of-life. Thus seeking harmony, we find peace. In *The Windwalker* this belief is brought out magnificently. The book is written with a reverent approach which is apparent even in the battle between the old man and the grizzly, where the reader feels the true meaning of this harmony and peace.

Similarly reverent is the approach as the old man talks with Giver-of-life. He presents himself in the second person, as a friend making an introduction to another. In truth the friend is himself. For our people this method conveys respect. This is how they offer themselves in prayer. A first-person approach to Deity would not be reverent.

Although *The Windwalker* personifies the philosophy of life of the Plains Indians in the story of an old man, it is more than that. It is a story of age, its wisdom and its memories, a story of teaching, humor, suffering, triumph, love, and peace. Thus it is essentially a story about each of us. In writing it, Blaine Yorgason has evidenced a remarkable ability to see life outside his own culture and then portray the other culture with profound dignity and insight in simple but powerful expression.

JOHN C. RAINER, JR.
Taos Pueblo — Creek — Cheyenne
VERENDA DOSELA RAINER
San Carlos Apache

Part One

The Scaffold

In total darkness and in total desperation the old man struggled against the cords which held him bound. In an agony of aching limbs he twisted his emaciated body back and forth, back and forth, straining with all the strength of a great spirit against an unseen enemy which would not release its hold.

And as his old body fought, so too did his mind, fighting through a choking, strangling fear of the unknown in the hope of finding understanding.

Oh, how he wished for his eyes, for the sight that had slipped from him while the seasons piled their weight upon his shoulders! And if not for his sight, then at least for the use of his hands, his friends, the warriors of his soul who had now become his second eyes. Yet they too were bound, anchored at his sides, and try as he would he could not work them loose.

In frustration and pain and fear he struggled, and as he fought the first tears started from his sightless old eyes and flowed down the creases of his skin where they mingled with the water from the melting snow.

And so that much he knew. It was snowing, he was bound tightly within a buffalo robe, and he was not within the lodge of his grandson, Smiling Wolf, the lodge where he had been when last he remembered.

Sheetshe! he cried aloud as he twisted his leathery face away from the icy blasts. This was bad! Very bad! Could this be what it was like in the land of the Sky People? But if it were, and he were there, then where were the deep blue skies, the green hills with bright streams wandering between them, the vast herds of buffalo, and the sacred hoops, the lodges of his people? And if he were there, why was the wind so cold against his face?

Another icy blast raked across the old man's shivering frame, and as it subsided he could hear the whispering of the snow drifting along the ground below, swirling around the small piles of rocks that supported the poles of the scaffold.

Scaffold! Could it be?

Yes, it had to be!

He was on the scaffold of the dead! And now the old man grunted in shock and fear as sudden memory swept across his mind.

It had been his day to die, the day that he had looked forward to and yet had feared for so many long seasons. He had sung his song of farewell for those few who might have cared to listen, and then he had lain back to await his departure into the west, into the land of the Sky People where the black road of his troubles was to end.

The old man thought for a moment, wondering how he could have been so wrong. He had thought he was on that road, he had thought that he was about to walk away on the wind. It was obvious that others too felt him dead. Thus he was on scaffold. Yet he was not dead, but was in fact very much alive, and now he must determine what to do.

Hoka-hey! he suddenly shouted into the wind, grinning widely as he shouted.

Hoka-hey, Grandfather!
This is a good joke you have
played.
A very good joke.

You have played many, but this
is the best, and
the old man who lies on this scaffold
salutes you.

For a moment he paused, wondering if the Great Wanken tanka, the great God, the one he called Grandfather, could even hear with the wind howling so loudly. Yet the cry of the wind should not stop the ears of Wanken tanka, no, not even a fierce wind like this one. He would hear, and now this great but painful joke would come to an end.

Grandfather,
though you do not feel it, the wind here
is cold,
and bound as this body which you have created is
to this scaffold,
it is unable to build a fire for
warmth.
Therefore, let us end this joke,
that this old man who wishes
to die
may continue his journey
to the west.
These eyes see only
darkness,
these ears are good for little except getting
cold,
these fingers ache and are no longer
nimble,
and these feet move more slowly than the season of
hunger.
Grandfather,
the weight of many winters is upon
this old back,
and it is in this man who lies before you to say,
this is a good day
to die.

Expectantly then, the old man closed his eyes and straightened his chin, and for many minutes not a single muscle on his aching body moved. But death did not come—no, would not come—not even when it was so greatly desired. So after a little the old man grunted in an agony of cold and began struggling once more.

Straining hard against the leather thongs that bound him, he continued the excruciating ordeal of trying to work his arms free. He would breathe deeply and then exhale all the air he possibly could, using the tiny space his hollow chest created as a place to move his arms. For many long moments he strained against the rawhide cords, and though the pain was great, he did his best to conceal even from himself his knowledge of the agony he felt.

At last, however, he was forced to stop. The cords were wrapped too tightly around his shoulders, he could not work his arms beyond that point, and the pain made further movement almost unbearable.

Ah, Grandfather, he groaned, trying to soothe his burning lungs and aching arms.
Give this old man the strength to free
his limbs;
either that, or free his
spirit.

Then he lay still, thinking. His bones were brittle, and he had to be careful about them. Still, if he was going to get to the ground, he had little choice. He was going to have to—

Suddenly his breath stilled. At first he wanted to doubt his old ears, to wipe out the memory of the sound he heard. But then it came again, a lonely, eerie howling that was at once a part of the wind and yet distinct from it. Almost instantly the cry was taken up from another quarter, and now the old man knew.

With terror mounting in his chest he waited, and moments later, when the sound came again, he was certain that it was nearer, much nearer.

Now, in an agony of heart that was so much more than cold and pain, he began to tense and untense the muscles in his body, straining back and forth, leaning with all his will first one way and then another. In a short time the scaffold crashed to the ground and the old man convulsed in pain, his breath driven from his chest when he hit.

Sheetshe, Mother Earth, he gasped, struggling desperately for air,
when last we touched your
breast was soft,
moist and pliable
as a mother's breast is
to her
children.
But now this old man feels only
your bones,
hard and unyielding, cold and
cruel.
Have you then
joined
with Old Man Winter,
and the hunger of the wolves,
to make this
battle
more difficult?
Dho! One hopes not!
This old body hurts too much
already.

Desperately he sucked in breath after breath, trying to straighten out his decrepit and timeworn body that screamed in agony with each movement he made. Yet the howling of the wolves made his fear overcome even the pain, and it was not many moments before he pulled himself with a great heaving from the bound-up buffalo robe and collapsed scaffold. Gasping and trembling then from both fear and cold, he began a frenzied effort to free the half-frozen robe.

Under the best of conditions it would have been painful

work for his age-bound fingers, but with snow and ice frozen into the hide he soon felt himself to be in a kind of endless agony. Because his eyes were dead, he was forced to rely on feeling, and the cold of the wind was so intense that he quickly lost any semblance of that. And to make matters worse, the howling on the wind was getting ever closer.

Grandfather, he wailed in desperation, his hands beating a tattoo against his thighs in an effort to restore circulation.

> *O Great Wanken tanka,*
> *once already this old man has explained that*
> *the weight of his winters is heavy*
> *upon him,* ·
> *and his old bones*
> *creak*
> *in the cold.*
> *His fingers are not able to free*
> *this robe,*
> *and his spirit longs to slip from*
> *his withered frame:*
> *Why is it,*
> *then,*
> *that he must live?*
> *May he not just lie back*
> *and die?*

The old man, still fumbling with the cords and poles of the scaffold, paused in his wailing to listen again to the fearful message on the wind. Oh, how the howlings of those wolves terrified him! If only he could see! If only his eyes were alive, that he might stand and do battle! But he could not see, he could not fight, and he knew that if the wolves found him he would be at the mercy of their savage hunger. He had seen such a battle once, and the memory of it would never leave him.

> *O Great Wanken tanka,*
> *where are the*
> *eyes*

of this old warrior,
and where is his
strength?
Time has robbed him of these,
and now do you expect him
to battle
without them?
Sheetshe! That is bad!
Can you not give him back
his eyes?
Can you not give him back
his years?
Where is the
justice
this warrior has heard of
so often?

Yes, he thought, and the icy wind made things even worse, for his withered body was now so cold that he had little control over it, little control at all. How could a blind old man like he—

Grandfather! he wailed once more, shouting into the wind in an effort to build his courage,
Old Man Winter
has blown in on his cloud
from the north
and has bedded down on the
mountaintops,
covering them with his robes of
snow.
His ice-bound fingers
have reached down onto the hill
where this old man sits,
stealing away the life from his
limbs
and holding all he touches in
his grip of death.
His breath is roaring from
his lips,

pelting
Mother Earth with
snow,
making her soft brown soil hard,
like the rocks,
and soon he will curl up and go to
sleep,
drawing all things into himself,
all things but the
cold
and the wolves.
    Grandfather,
this old man who sits before you
has seen,
already,
more snows and more grasses than a man
should see.
His eyes are long dead,
his ears are not as they
should be.
His limbs shake even when he has done
no work,
and pain gnaws at them continually.
His only purpose seems to be
consuming food,
food that he can no longer
provide
for himself,
food that a dutiful grandson
must provide.
    You see, Grandfather,
this old creature is but a
burden, a burden upon
the life of his
grandson.
To the wives of his grandson he is only
more work,
and to their children he is
nothing,

nothing at all.
  O Mighty One,
let this old body nourish
Mother Earth!
Let this spirit
walk up on the wind into the land
of the Sky People.
O Great Wanken tanka,
do you hear?

In answer the winds howled more fiercely than ever around the hilltop, and now the old man's body began to shake even more violently with the cold. As long as he could he sat in silence, his bony old shoulders hunched against the wind, but suddenly he sat up with a start, listening. He could hear them again, he could hear their hungry cries blowing past him. Once more he clawed at the frozen robe, knowing he needed its warmth, yet fearing to work any longer trying to obtain it. The wolves were nearer, much nearer, and already he seemed to feel their razor-sharp fangs tearing at his flesh.

In terror he struggled to his feet, turning first one way and then another, straining to hear the wolves, straining to know if—

And then his foot slipped on an icy rock and he fell heavily, awkwardly, into the snow. Desperately he lunged to his feet once more, turning to run, and as he did so he tripped in his blindness and again fell to the earth, striking his forehead painfully against the rocks that had supported the scaffold.

  O Great God, he wailed through the screaming wind, doing his best to control his pent-up emotions.
Why? Why must
an old man
suffer so?
All his days this man has
feared death,
and now on the day when
courage to die has finally
come,

death has blown away on
the wind,
leaving him
alone
to suffer
once more.
Sheetshe, O Great One,
if you wish this
weary old man to
die,
then let it be quickly,
and not by his
brothers
the wolves,
or by Old Man Winter.
If you wish him to
live,
then—

And the old man, groping forward in the snow, suddenly felt beneath his hand the shaft of his war lance, the lance he had so carefully crafted many seasons before.

With a feeling of wonder he pulled it to him, and then he sat running his fingers back and forth along the chipped stone point, thinking deeply as he did so.

Ah, Great Man Above, he finally murmured,
is this the way it is
to be?
Do you show this old
creation
the lance
that he might do battle?
Dho, one hopes not!
One does not battle
in his blindness,
or on top of the mountain
of his years.
Yet the lance is here,

and this tired old warrior
wonders how—

   And then another blast of wind and snow slammed against
the old man, hitting with such force that he was almost
toppled over. Hastily he turned and ducked his head, doing
his best to avoid the icy fury of the storm. And as he did so he
felt before him the frozen buffalo robe he had abandoned only
moments before.

   For an instant there was no comprehension, then with a
look of awe he lifted his wrinkled face to the sky.

   Grandfather,
this old person has angered you.
That was not his
intention,
and he feels great
regret.
You have shown him his lance—
and now the robe.
His body shakes even more with the
cold,
which is the way his body chooses
to tell him that he is being
an old fool, and that he
must get busy.
   Grandfather,
this man finds it a clear
and happy thought,
thinking that you have used his
old body
once again to teach him, as you have so often
before, with happiness and pleasure,
sorrow and
pain,
the lessons you would have him
learn.

   Quickly then the old man set about cutting the bonds which

held the robe. His lance, chipped to a fine serrated edge, cut the thongs easily, and so the man moved rapidly from cord to cord, wondering as he worked that God should want him to remain alive.

The wind still slammed furiously against him, and the snow flew before it, drifting into ridges and sifting into and through any opening its seeking and probing fingers could find.

Yet the old man closed his mind against the gripping and biting teeth of the snow and wind, steeling his body against it as he forced himself to think of nothing except freeing the robe and then fleeing before the wind. And the howling of the wolves came to his ears again, now close, now far away, but always there, always there.

Terror gripped his spirit as he redoubled his efforts to cut the robe free, furiously sawing while his mind darted rapidly from the wolves to wonderment about his life and back to the wolves.

Suddenly the robe pulled loose, and instantly the old man was on his feet and moving across the top of the hill, the robe held behind to protect him from the pounding of the wind.

And as he stumbled forward he prayed into the wind, his prayers more random snatches of thought than organized supplications. Yet prayers they were, of questions not understood and of fears not under control.

O Great One,
this person is old,
his eyes are long dead,
and people have
no idea
what a blind old warrior
is good for.
Sheetshe!
Neither has he.
Yet he wishes to learn.
Grandfather,
we both understand that this old body
can do very little
any more.

But maybe to be needed a man
does not have to do
something.
Maybe he can just be there,
like a star in the nations above,
for others to take
their direction
from.
Is that to be the purpose of
this old man?
If so, then he is willing.

But, Grandfather, he added, doing his best to smile,
this old man you have created would ask a favor,
very small.
When a fire glows it does so because
of warmth.
If you wish this creation of yours
to glow,
then perhaps you will
hold back his brothers
the wolves
and help him
get warm.

Once more he wondered how such an old one as he could be
expected to do anything. What more could there possibly be?
What could be left to learn? What could be left to do? What
could—

One other favor, O Great One.
When it is time,
will you tell this old man why?

Part Two

The Cave

With tottering steps the old man anxiously made his way down the steep slope of the hill, keenly aware of the nearness of the wolves. The snow, only a foot deep, was just high enough to cover most of the rocks. And these, with their icy surfaces, proved most treacherous.

In his haste his feet slipped constantly, and often he slammed heavily into the drifting snow. After several such falls, as he was climbing shakily to his feet, he paused with sudden realization. Then, with a feeling of awe, he lifted his face once more to the snow-shrouded sky.

Grandfather,
this man is humbled again by your
constant kindness,
and his old heart beats with
gratitude.
You help this body to move by making it
so cold
that it must. And then,

knowing that old legs are frail
and shake with age,
you, O Wise One, provide the snow
to soften their
falling.

And so, with the wind and the snow swirling around him, the old Indian gripped the almost useless buffalo robe tightly and continued groping his way to the bottom of the hill. Once there, he moved resolutely forward into the darkness of his life, feeling his way ahead as carefully as possible.

Often he fell, and not infrequently he suffered severe pain as his bony legs slammed against a rock or his head against a low-hanging tree limb. Yet he forced himself to ignore the agony as he pushed forward, ever forward, trying desperately in his blindness to find his family as he fled from the hunger of the wolves.

Though it was impossible to tell with any certainty, the old warrior had the feeling that he was in the same valley where his grandson and the rest of the village had placed their lodges. But if that were true, he wondered, then in which direction must he go to find them?

In the lee of a lightning-blasted pine he paused to rub the numbness out of his body, catch his breath, and consider his choices. He could hear the stream directly before him, and he knew that he could now go in either direction and have an equal chance of finding his people. And perhaps the sacred hoop of lodges would still be there. Yet within his heart the old man feared that all of the people, including his family, would be gone. He knew from long years the customs and the traditions of his people, and he knew as well as they did that it was never wise to remain long in a place of death. As well, his own family would have begun their wandering so that they might mourn his passing in a proper manner.

O Great Wanken tanka, he groaned aloud,
how we have all
been fooled!
What is the purpose in

this, that this old man is dead to all
but himself?
Would it not have been
better
if the bones of his youth,
had been scattered about on
the prairie
to show where a warrior
had fallen,
and to make a story?
   Grandfather,
this man has tried, but as yet
he cannot see
where it is good
to grow old.

For several moments the old man rested against the tree, staring with his sightless eyes out into the snow-filled valley. The wind had now grown quiet enough that he could hear the whispering of the snow as it drifted over the ground, seeking out and filling the hollows and low spots, making the whole world seem flat and smooth. The faint sound brought back memories, and for a moment or so he was in another time, another place.

The snow is so
beautiful, O Great One.
How could this old man have forgotten
how beautiful
it is? See, one remembers that it turns
the meadow grass
into giant eagle feathers,
and bends the pines low
in humility
with its weight.
   Out there some geese are flying past,
late on their journey.
Do you hear?
Though these old eyes

cannot see them now,
they have seen, through the
seasons,
many such, and they know,
O Great One,
that the sky is the same
color
as the underside of their wings.
    Ah, Grandfather,
could anything be more beautiful,
more pure?
Do you show this beauty
to cause an old man
to wonder
how he can bear to die
and leave this lovely creation?
Dho! Of course you do!
Like the pines, this man is
bent low, in humility,
and it is a good feeling
to have.
The snow has made all things
white
and clean. Perhaps
it will do the same
for him.

Onward then he struggled, on through the freezing, drifting snow. Oh, how his legs ached! They were trembling so badly that he wondered how he could go any farther, any farther at all. And his chest! He had never felt such burning pain! Would it never end? Could he never stop? It had been some time since he had heard the sound of the wolves, but the old warrior knew that meant little. They were behind him. Yes, and they were still hungry.

Sheetshe, he groaned as he pushed himself through a clump of trees he had stumbled into,

since the eyes of this old warrior
died
he has never ventured
far alone
upon any path,
no matter how familiar.
    How, Grandfather, can he expect
to flee when there is
no path, no,
nor sight to
find one.
    Dho—

And the aged warrior suddenly cried out as he stumbled
over an old windfall and tumbled into the snow, a jagged
branch slashing through his leggings and into his thigh. It was
several breaths before the man realized what had happened.
But when he felt the warm blood trickling down his leg and
into the snow he panicked, hacking frantically at the buffalo
robe, fearing not so much the wound as that the smell of
blood, his blood, would drive the wolves into a killing frenzy.
In an agony of fear he tied a strip of hide about his thigh,
struggled to his feet, and fled.

The man heard no sound as he moved, no sound but the
swishing of his feet through the snow. That, and the murmur
of the nearly frozen stream, the crying of the wind in the
pines, and, yes, he was sure he could hear the howling on the
wind once again.

He was out of the trees now, almost running as he moved
across a gradually sloping meadow. Constantly the meadow-
grass tugged at his ankles and feet, and tiny ice-crystals tore
like knives at this leggings and moccasins, gradually cutting
thin the finely tanned leather from which they had been made.

O Grandfather, he groaned, as he stumbled forward,
do not let these brothers
the wolves
scent the blood-smell

of this old man.
    Do not let them—

Often now he put snow in his mouth, soothing with its coolness his tortured lungs and throat, and as well as he could he held snow against his wound, hoping the cold would slow the bleeding. Yes, and—

With a grunt of surprise the old man toppled over a bank, and as he smashed through the ice and into the freezing water of a beaver pond he felt his breath driven from him in a rush of bunching muscles, muscles constricted by the freezing water.

For a moment he was certain he would drown, but then he realized that the water was not deep. Struggling to his feet he reached out with his lance, found the bank, pushed his way to it and pulled himself out of the icy pond.

Now his tired old body was shaking violently, and he could never remember being so cold or feeling so lost and so alone.

O Great One, he sobbed as he struggled to his feet, wringing as much freezing water as possible from his leather clothing,
why,
why is this old man
suffering
when he has traveled
so far
along the dark road
of his troubles?
Does there not come
a time
when one has
suffered
enough?
What good can come of
such suffering
now?
Does there not come
a time
when the dark road
ends?

When a man
at last
finds happiness
and peace?
You gave this man the lance,
O Great One,
that he might
live.
Yet you also allowed him
to stumble
and feel all over his frame
the icy grip of
the stream, an icy grip
that will bring death
quickly
on a day such as this.
There is also the
blood, warm from
the wound
in this leg,
and now, no doubt,
flowing too from these
old feet
where the moccasins
have worn away.
In what better way
could a warrior
leave
a trail
for his brothers
the wolves?
*   O Grandfather,*
what would you have
this son of yours do?
Yes, and where
would you have
him go?
His mind longs for
death

and yet fears it as greatly
as his frame must.
For though his legs are tired
and feeble,
and shake with the cold,
yet they fight on,
carrying him forward.
This old warrior is unable to walk
as fast as he once did,
or as far,
but he can walk,
and still does.
Why is it that
his legs, his arms,
his feet, his hands,
and his mind
continue to fight
on and on
against death,
when it should be
so welcome,
so pleasant?

Through the afternoon the old warrior made his way slowly and painfully through the grass and snow and over the rocks of the valley floor, moving constantly to keep warm and to escape the wolves, searching in vain with his ears and his feet for something that he might recognize, some sign that the lodges of his people were near. Though the snow had stopped falling and the wind was less violent, the sky was still overcast and threatening, and the old man could feel the chill of the storm upon his cheek. Soon, he knew, he would have to find shelter, he would have to find warmth.

The whispering stillness was profound, and he found himself fighting a growing sense of loneliness. Yet now it was there, and to ease its haunting pain he spent more and more of the afternoon discussing his thoughts vocally with his God, the Great Creator, the first Father, Wanken tanka. In all his life the old warrior had never spoken so directly nor so frequently to this great Being, always viewing himself as unworthy to do so. But now, somehow, all that had changed. He had been on his way, he felt, to the land of spirits, and then for some reason had been called back. That seemed to give him the right to intimate communication. And so, as he stumbled forward through the afternoon, he spoke with his quiet and quavering voice of the thoughts that plucked at his mind, and of the feelings and fears that brushed against his heart, sharing himself and thinking more deeply than ever he had before.

As he made his way through the snow, he was amazed that he could be so cold, so nearly dead, his body in such agony, and yet have his mind wander backward along the pathways of his life the way it was doing. Those pathways, he knew, had been rarely trod, and then not for many seasons. Yet now he walked them easily, and he wondered at it.

He thought of the days of his youth when his arrows found the life of the fleet antelope and of the high-climbing sheep. He thought of sitting within his lodge as he watched his mother prepare the wasna from the buffalo his father had killed. He felt again the stirrings within his breast as he first gazed upon Tashina, the young woman who would be his wife. And he recalled the heaviness of spirit, the totally help-less feeling that had been his as he pulled the lifeless body of his first-born, his son Little Bear, from beneath the murky waters of the river. Oh, the loneliness of that day! The bitter irony of life, that one so young could never know the joys other men had known.

And now his memories flew forward to that other day, the day his mind fled always from, the day that the Crow warriors had found his Tashina alone gathering berries. Even now, after such a long time, he felt the tears start in his eyes as he thought of the heartache that had been his, the loneliness that had started the moment he found her dead and broken frame, the loneliness that still continued to haunt him.

Quickly he forced his mind away from Tashina, bringing it forward to his struggles through the snow and to his freezing and starving and nearly dead old body. Intently then he strained his ears. Again he could hear nothing, nothing but the wind and the sounds of his fleeing and his labored breathing. Where were the wolves? Where was the sound of their coming? Where were—

His mind was away again, away on a long-ago war party when he had first learned of his own courage. From there he thought of his daughter, and of how many horses she had been worth to the brave who finally won her. On and on his thoughts drifted, going back and forth over the years as though the seasons did not exist at all, as though all time were the same and it was all one day.

Grandfather, he murmured,
how is it that
so many seasons have
flown by,
passing so quickly
across this man's
life,
almost without his being
aware
of their going?
When he takes a drink
at the stream,
the face gazing at him
from out of the water
is a stranger to him.
That face is wrinkled and creased.
It shows a stooped old man, one who must use
three legs.
He has on his head
the white war bonnet,
hair as white as the winter snow,
thinning
until there is almost not enough of it
to braid.
    O Great One,
this man sees this image in his mind and he knows
it is himself, yet at the same time his spirit
cries out,
Wait!

That wrinkled frame is not him at all,
but is instead simply a
prison,
a clay prison within which the young man
that he is
struggles for release.
*   And, Grandfather,*
most interesting of all
is how this man feels.
He knows he is
what others call
old,
for he has seen many winters
pass him by.
Yet somehow
he feels no different than he did
that clear morning when he first leaped,
unaided,
to the back of his buffalo runner.
His heart, his spirit,
is the same now
as it was then.
Though his eyes do not see,
his heart still leaps with joy
when it sees in memory his beautiful
woman,
or hears her voice,
or feels her softness.
It thrills when it recalls the sun
burning the clouds in the afternoon
sky.
It still cries with sorrow
when it hears needless
pain
or learns of
senseless brutality.
It still beats with wonder
as it observes the birth of a
child,

or the rebirth of Mother Earth as she greens
to life
when the time of cold is past.
  What this man who stands before you is saying,
O Great One,
is that he always thought,
when he was young,
that he would feel old when he reached
thirty winters,
or fifty winters,
or even eighty winters.
Strangely, now that he has passed even these,
he does not feel old at all.

Here he paused for a moment, grinning a little, then he continued.

  He should say, Grandfather,
that he does not feel old
until his bones
begin to ache with
the cold.
Then he feels old!
Still, this old frame within which
he dwells
is his friend,
and does its best
to keep up with him.
There have been many times
when he has not treated it
well,
yet it has forgiven him
of a great deal.
He should not be so unhappy
with it.
When the children of his grandson Smiling Wolf
look away with contempt,
or pity,
then he should say, Do not worry,

old friend.
They do not understand the
battles
you have fought daily
for so many long seasons.
Soon, though, they will understand,
for age comes
to all, even children,
one sunrise at a time.
And it will come to them,.
each of them,
with as much
surprise
and swiftness
as it came to you.
Dho, yes, when
one recalls—

Suddenly across the old man's senses swarmed the haunting, chilling sound of the wolves, much nearer. And the man
knew their cries were different, too, the sound was more
excited, more full of anticipation. They had found his trail!
They had found the blood from his wound.

O Great Man above, he cried in agony and terror, *do not let*
these brothers the wolves—

And he thought suddenly of the day he sat on the side of a
hill watching a pack of wolves hunting below him. They had
found a moose, a strong young male, and he watched in
amazement and not a little awe as they circled it, taking turns
feigning an attack while they wore down the strength of the
helpless animal. Then, as if on some prearranged signal, two
of the wolves leaped for its head, distracting the attention of
the moose. And in that instant of distraction another wolf
leaped in behind and slashed the hamstrings on the moose's
hind legs, totally crippling it. From that instant it had been
only a matter of time, only a game that the wolves were
playing, only—

In a frenzy of fear the old man floundered forward through
the snow, pushing, praying, pleading. Only—

Again came the lonesome howling, so close now. So close. Almost instantly he heard a series of short coughs and growls and with a chilling realization the old warrior knew it would do no good to run any farther. Far better to stand and face them, doing battle as best he could, making the price they paid for his life as dear to them as possible.

Quickly then he rose to his feet and turned, holding his lance out before him. Oh, how he longed for his eyes, for the vision that had been taken from him. How many were there? he wondered, and where were they? How close were they?

Strangely, now that the wolves had found him he felt no animosity toward them, no enmity at all. They were simply animals, hungry brothers doing all they could to survive.

Dho, Brothers, he shouted, doing his best to keep his fear from leaping into his voice.

Of all the things this old man has wished
to consider,
the thoughts of your hunger
were not among them.

Loudly he began to sing his courage song, lifting his feet slowly up and down as he pointed the lance first one way, then another, turning slowly in a circle as he tried to tell from which direction the attack would come.

And now his thoughts flew off once more, flying back to a time of struggle when his grandfather had counseled him.

My son,
a true man must learn to be
many things at
many times.
Often he will have need
for fierceness,
like our brother, the bear
But just as often he will have need
for gentleness,
like our sister the
butterfly.

There will be times when he must be
as a mountain,
straight and tall,
his eyes seeing everywhere
at once.
But there will also be times
when he must be
as a valley,
silent and blind to all.
And there will always be times,
hard times,
when a man should be as an eagle.
Then he can mount the wind,
higher and higher,
until he suddenly sees
how small
everything truly is.
Then he can smile and
return,
and things won't seem so hard.
Then he can—

And in that instant the wolves rushed, silently and yet so swiftly that the old warrior had no time to think, no time to prepare except to lift his lance a little higher as he heard their footfalls.

He was first hit from behind and knocked forward. As he fell he thrust his lance forward and felt it strike flesh. Then something like hot fire took hold of his arm and he was down and rolling in the snow and there were warm bodies and he was thrusting and swinging with his lance and kicking and the foul smell of the wolves was almost more than he could bear.

He wondered as he struggled that he felt no pain, for he could hear their teeth snapping and knew that at least one of the wolves was tearing at his leg. He was also aware that in his twisting and fighting the buffalo robe had become wrapped around him. With sudden realization he understood that the robe had, by covering his head and neck, probably saved his life. And as that thought flashed through his mind he felt the

robe savagely yanked from him. Desperately he pulled himself around, groping for the lost robe, reaching. Suddenly a
wolf's body was across his face and he screamed and shoved
at it with his empty hand, pushing with all his might, and then
his foot found another one and suddenly he was alone.

For an instant he lay still, listening to the savage growling
and fighting that was going on near him. What had happened? Somehow for the moment they had lost him. The
wolves were fighting over something else, and he was alone.
The robe! Of course! The robe had his blood upon it, and the
wolves must have become confused about what they were
after! Instantly the man began to pull himself through the
snow, trying to get away from them, still fighting for his life
even when part of his mind kept telling him how hopeless it
was.

Before him was a fallen log, its ancient branches reaching up
to block his way. In an agony of fear he pushed his way
through them, thrusting his lance before him as he dragged
himself over the rotting tree, getting as far away as possible,
getting—

And now there was another windfall, another tree in his
way. As he pushed his body over that one he heard the rush of
feet and felt the fangs tear through his leggings and into his
leg.

Instantly he lashed out with his other foot and shoved
against the wolf, and then he was over the other log and
rolling and—

Suddenly he felt the snow give way beneath him. Wildly he
reached out, grabbing, but there was nothing to hold to and he
fell, landing heavily in soft earth several feet below.

For a moment he lay still, listening to the savage snarling
directly above him. But suddenly it ended in yelps that
sounded like fear to him and then he was alone again, staring
into the inky blackness of his blindness. Slowly, gradually, he
became aware that the air around him was warmer, that he
was out of the wind, and that he was not so alone as he
thought.

With his old heart in his throat he whispered a greeting, but
when several queries brought no response, he began to inch

his way toward the sounds he heard, the sounds of heavy breathing.

He crawled very cautiously, yet even then he froze in terror when his hand rested not on earth but on a fur-covered body. And he would have fled instantly had his old legs been able to support him or had there been anywhere to flee to.

As it was, the shock of the experience was more than his drained and aged body could tolerate, and the old man simply fainted dead away, his chilled body slumping to the earth next to the hibernating grizzly his groping fingers had found.

Part Three

The Grizzly and the Horse

Many hours passed before the old man at last opened his sightless eyes. For a long moment he stared into his blindness, trying to understand where he was. Oh, how he ached! Every bone and muscle throbbed with a will of its own, and he could never remember being so sore. Then realization flooded upon him and he hurriedly began inching away from the warm body against which he had been lying.

Moments later he was as far away from the giant bear as he could get—no more than four or five steps—and he was even more aware of the precariousness of his situation. His probing fingers quickly told him that he was in a cave that was not so much a cave as it was an overhanging bank supported by the roots of a great tree. Across that overhang several other trees had fallen, the years had deposited leaves and other debris, the storm had laid down between two and three feet of snow, and now the whole mass formed a very effective cave indeed. Despite his groping search, the man could find no way out except for the small hole, now mostly covered, through which he had fallen. And try as he would, and as desperately as he wanted to, he could not muster the strength to leap up to the hole.

With a feeling of stark terror gripping his heart, he faced the sleeping bear. Somehow he knew that it was large, even for a grizzly. Also, for some reason he was certain that it was a male. The bear seemed to be sleeping soundly, yet still the old man huddled against the dirt bank as far from it as he could get. Of all his four-footed brothers, this one only did he truly fear, and this one he feared with all his heart.

Many times during his long life he had felt fear, but always before he had only to recall the vision of his youth and touch the sacred bundle hung around his neck and that fear would be gone. Then he would be full of power and courage, signs of the true man. But now he felt no power, no courage, only the cold hand of fear that was clenched around his entrails, the cold hand that had gripped him constantly since he had awakened on the scaffold.

Over and over he touched the sacred bundle, but always when he sent his thoughts back to his vision they would somehow get lost and wander over to the willows along the stream where he and his brother-friend, Crooked Horse, were playing games. What a clear day that had been, with the sun warm upon the earth and the willows thick and green with new leaves! The stream was singing a new song, a song of joy, and he sang with it, for never had he felt so alive. At first they had wrestled, he and Crooked Horse, and then each disappeared into the willows to see who could capture the other. It was almost instantly that he heard the screaming. Terrified, he turned and rushed through the heavy growth toward the sound. Suddenly he burst into a tiny clearing and there he found his brother-friend, Crooked Horse, groaning in death. The giant grizzly quickly brushed aside the body of his friend and charged, and as though it were only one sun ago he could feel the white-hot slash as a monstrous paw raked his ribs, sending him reeling into the willows. Then with a searing and crushing pain he felt the powerful jaws close upon his shoulder and lift him into the air. From that time he had known nothing until the day he opened his eyes within the

Lakota lodge to gaze into the face of Tashina, the one who would one day become his woman.

For years he had lived that experience over and over in his dreams, and now the terrible wounds that were in his mind had opened once more. How, he wondered, could he be expected to go through all that again?

Then, just as the light faded from the cave and the sun sank into the earth, the bear stirred. For a moment or so it snorted and grunted, and then it rolled over to its other side where it finally settled down again.

The old man, terror-stricken, cowered against the dirt bank, and it was not until his senses began reeling that he realized he was holding his breath. Slowly he exhaled, carefully struggling to do it as silently as possible. For some reason the bear stirred around several times during the next few hours, and each grunt and movement drove a new flood of terror over the old man.

Before dawn, sick, exhausted, and fearing that his end was near, he finally dozed off. Suddenly he was no longer in the cave, he was no longer a blind old man, and it was no longer the moon of dark red calves. Instead he was a youth and it was the moon when cherry stones hardened and he was standing with his body painted all over in the sacred color of red and he was trembling with fear and exhaustion. For three days, from sunrise to the time of its setting, he had danced the sun dance, blinding himself as he stared into the sun each day as it slowly trailed across the sky. Now he stood quaking with fear as the holy man sliced his breasts and inserted the leather thongs he was supposed to slowly tear himself away from. At first he felt no pain, but as the drums began and he leaned back with their rhythm against the thongs, all the pain in the world seemed to center upon his breasts. He forgot about the dance, he forgot about his desire for a vision, he forgot about everything but the pain. It felt like someone was pulling the raw heart out of his chest. He wanted to cry out and drop to the earth and die, but somehow he found the strength to dance, to dance and to keep on dancing.

This seemed always, only suddenly it was not and the world had gone dark. He was spinning, spinning and falling, and it was so dark, with nothing he could hold to, nothing at all. And now he felt again the fear knot up in his belly as he fell around and around, down and down.

And this too seemed always until it wasn't and he was no longer falling. He was still spinning, but he was suddenly in the form of a hoop, rolling on and on, over many grasses and over many snows, all alone in a wide, flat world. Still he felt the fear, and now with it the pain came again, agonizing and overpowering, constant and burning, driving his heart into his throat until he thought he would die with it.

Then suddenly he was not alone, but was rolling beside another hoop, this one bathed in a pure white light. As he saw the other hoop his pain and fear vanished and he felt a calmness, a calmness so total and so complete that he realized instantly who the clear hoop was. The clear and sacred hoop was the Grandfather, the Great Wanken tanka, the God of all, who had come to travel with him.

On they traveled, on and on, and it seemed there was no end to the seasons they crossed. Occasionally they would start to separate, and each time that happened the pain and fear would return. Pleadingly he would call to the Grandfather, who would come close again, driving the pain and the fear away.

When this had happened many times, the man began to wonder why it was so, and as the wonder formed a thought in his mind, the clear sacred hoop vanished and a red eagle appeared, sailing down to land in a tree against which he himself stopped rolling.

Quietly then the eagle, who was once again Wanken tanka, spoke, teaching him the meaning of the sacred hoop or circle, a meaning which the warrior had never remembered. Many more things did the eagle teach him, but of these only one could the young dancer recall.

My son, the eagle said,
the life of a man is a happy
time,
but it is also a time
to suffer and endure.

Pain is able to teach
courage
and without courage there is nothing
good.
In times of fear and pain
the proud heart
dies,
and then the power of Wanken tanka
will come in
and live in that heart,
giving it the true courage that
fears nothing,
seeks not for praise,
and strives for the good of
all.
Give many thanks for fear and pain.
They are friends, and
they will be yours often,
often enough
that you will become
the man
you are to be.

Slowly the old man regained his senses, listening with one ear to the movements of the bear as he thought with his mind of his dream, of the dream he had now known twice. The dream was strong, full of power, and now as he thought about it he felt his body filling with the old strength, strength such as he felt in the dream whenever the clear sacred hoop that was Wanken tanka came near.

Ah, Grandfather,
when this man was a youth he was taught
that there would be many
hard things,
but that of them all, four would be
the hardest.
Getting food was the first,
for without food

there is nothing else.
The second hardest thing would be
losing his oldest child.
The third hardest thing would be
losing
his woman,
and the fourth hardest thing would be
fighting a big war party
when his own was small.
*   Over the years,*
O Great One,
this old man has known all of these.
And they are indeed hard.
Yet none of them is so hard as the battle
he fights now
to overcome the fear in his belly,
the fear that cripples.
These others he has done alone,
using the strength he has found
within himself.
But this fear
is more than he is,
and without you he is lost
to it.
*   Grandfather,*
in the days of his youth you gave this man
a dream,
and taught him this truth,
That without you, he is
nothing.
Now he has walked many roads,
some that were good,
some that were bad,
and he has passed over many
grasses
and many
snows.
He wears the white war bonnet,
his body is stooped and bent,

many of his teeth have been uprooted,
his eyes are dead,
and he must walk with three legs.
Is it not strange that in
the winter of his life
he must be called back from
the world of spirits
that he might learn again
this same truth?

For some time the man was silent, deep in thought. Daylight slowly crept into the hole and felt its way about the cave, and still the old man didn't move. The bear stirred once more, grunting a little, and the man seemed to pay it no mind, no mind at all. And then suddenly a grin spread across his wrinkled old face, and his eyes that could not see once again began to twinkle.

Very well, Grandfather,
this old man is beginning to find understanding.
Because he no longer hears so well
with his ears,
he is now learning to hear
with his heart,
and he finds that a clear and happy thought.
All things are directed by you,
O Great One,
for the good of your creations—
the two-footers,
the four-footers,
and all the wings of the air.
The older this man grows the more he understands
that we are all
brothers and sisters,
children of Maka,
the Mother Earth.
Our frames come from her,
and one day each of us
must return

our frames to her,
that we might more easily
travel
into the world of spirits,
where we will find
true happiness.
This is a thing that all hearts
desire greatly,
for the land of spirits is
a pleasant
and beautiful
place.
Yet, Grandfather,
you have taught that we all come here
with a purpose.
In your wisdom you have made a man
so that he will not
enter
into the world of spirits
until his purpose is
fulfilled.
If the air he breathes is
shut off,
he fights for more.
If he feels hunger or thirst
he searches until that need
is satisfied.
If he is set upon by an enemy,
he fights
with great strength
and determination
that he might preserve his
life.
This man's own life has crossed over
many seasons,
and lately he has longed for the world
of spirits
where Tashina
and all the friends of his youth

now dwell.
Yes, O Great One,
this man dislikes mightily
loneliness
and the pain it brings.
Yet he feels there must be more
to his life here, for he
clings to it
so desperately.
All his life has been a dance, a dance
and a song.
When he was young and
light upon the earth his steps were quick
and easy.
Now he is heavy upon the earth, and
his steps are slow, halting
and difficult.
But his dance is still strong within him, and
still he sings his song.
His song is of the air
he breathes,
his song is of the memory of the great boulders
in his life,
his song is what he hears and feels
in his heart,
his song insists
that he will never die.
And now his old frame too sings
a song,
an aching song of
wounds untended,
an aching song of hunger.
You see how he is clinging to life?
It is not the season for berries;
this man has no wasna and no papa,
nor has he a lodge
with the juicy hump of a fat buffalo cow
roasting
on the fire.

Yet, Grandfather,
there lies a brother,
the bear,
sleeping and awaiting his entry
into
the world of spirits.
On him there is much meat,
and his coat will easily keep an old man
warm.
This man sees now, with his heart, that it was no
accident
that brought him to
this den.
Be close to this old warrior, therefore,
that he might have
the courage to do what must be
done.

Carefully then the old man felt around on the underside of the trees until he found shreds of the soft inner bark of the cottonwood. This he worked with his hands until he was satisfied it was right. Next he took snow and cleaned the wounds on his arm and leg, and then he bound the bark to them with what was left of his leggings.

Now he felt around until he found his lance, which he had somehow pulled into the den with him as he fell. The point had broken during the fall, so the old man patiently began chipping a new edge on it. He did not hurry because he could not, for all his speed had fled with his youth. Yet he worked well, and when at last he was finished he wondered that he should have done such a fine job when he might never use it again. Still, all things had a life of their own. He had enjoyed a strong frame. Should not his lance have the same joy?

Cautiously then the old man prepared to slay his brother the bear. He had no sacred pipe, so he held his hands as though the pipe was there, offering prayers to the four quarters of the earth and to Wanken tanka and to Maka, the mother of all. At last he made as if to set it down, stem toward where he felt the sunrise would be, dedicating it to Wanken tanka. Next he gave thanks to the grizzly, thanking it for its warmth, its courage, its strength and its life. Then he felt with his finger-eyes for the right spot on the bear. Now he was ready.

For a moment he stood still, calming his trembling limbs that perhaps did not yet know that he felt no fear. Then with all his strength he cried out, *Hoka-hey*, and drove his lance deep behind the right foreleg of the bear, seeking its heart.

At first the bear only grunted, but suddenly it lunged to its feet and with a mighty roar, it stood swaying back and forth. The old man, backing slowly away, listened in amazement as the giant grizzly growled in pain and anger while it stood batting at the lance in its side. Then with another roar it attacked the old tree, fiercely shredding the bark and wood with its claws. Suddenly it fell back to the earth, driving the lance in more deeply. Again it stood to attack the tree, and again it fell back upon the lance. Now the roaring was a continuous thing and in the midst of it the bear suddenly turned and began dragging itself straight toward the old man.

For an instant the warrior's heart leaped into his throat, but then before him he saw in his mind the clear sacred hoop that was Wanken tanka, and suddenly his fear was gone. Quietly he stood and faced the roaring grizzly, which slowly dragged its huge mass to where its swaying head was within inches of the man's chest.

The stench of its breath was fearsome, and blood and saliva flowed from its mouth onto the old man's tattered leggings and moccasins. Its huge mouth was open wide, and its teeth, yellowed and filthy, were larger that the aged warrior could have ever imagined.

There was a scream of terror in his throat, for the stench of the bear was full of evil memories, and he knew that he had to run, to flee. Yet somehow he kept his old feet firmly planted and knew that no sound escaped from between his lips.

Grandfather, he suddenly heard himself whispering, amid the fearsome roarings of the bear,
For the first time this man is
thankful
that his eyes do not

see
and that his ears do not
hear well,
for even with deafness and blindness this old man
is seeing and hearing more
than one can comfortably
enjoy.

For an everlastingly long time the bear roared in his face, only inches away and yet coming no closer. But life gradually left it and it sank to the floor of the cave where at last it was still. After many more moments the man carefully located his lance and removed it, and with its point he took the strong parts from within the bear, the favorite parts. These he ate raw, chewing each mouthful thoroughly. His several-day fast caused him to fill quickly, and when he could eat no more he lay back and slept. Upon awakening he ate again, and then he began the laborious task of removing the pelt.

For many days the old man remained in the cave, eating as he could, tending his wounds, tanning the pelt of the bear, and building up his strength. After two days of effort he got a fire going, and besides enjoying its warmth while it cooked his food, he let it eat away at the trees that formed his prison.

And then one day his hands found the opening, almost hidden, where the bear had entered the den, and at last he was free. Carefully he packed as much of the meat as he could carry. Then, wrapping the bear hide about him, he stooped and crawled out of the hole into the day.

Slowly he moved forward through the snow, his lance held before him to guide the way.

Suddenly he stopped. Yonder, somewhere close, was a horse. He could hear nothing, yet his nose told him that it was there, and he could not doubt that.

Straining his senses, he cautiously moved forward, but only when the animal finally nickered could he determine exactly where it was.

After many moments of waiting he hesitantly approached, thinking of the Crows. Only after long moments of careful feeling with his hands was he sure that the horse was alone, for it was not mounted, and there were no other tracks in the snow.

Gently the old man took hold of the fine rawhide cord that was around its neck, silently wondering as he did so that the horse was not terrified of the bearskin robe that he wore nor of the bear-smell that was about him. He could feel that the animal had been recently painted with the sacred hoop around its right eye to give it the power to see its way home. It also had battle markings on it, similar to the battle markings he had painted upon his own buffalo runner so long ago. Yet his fingers could find no ownership markings upon it, no indications that it belonged to anyone. There were none, that is, unless one thought of the medicine shield tied to its mane or the rawhide thong in its mouth. But now the old man wondered even more, for the rawhide thong, so far as he could tell, was new. So too was the medicine shield, but the markings on it, also fresh, felt like the same ones he had painted on his own shield so many seasons before.

For a moment only he hesitated, wondering, but then he grinned and, his decision made, the old man struggled onto the back of the buffalo runner. The horse turned and looked at him, much as if it were making certain that he was ready. Then gently it moved off through the snow, going down the canyon, carrying the old man forward.

Part Four

The Family

The old man could not remember the last time he had felt so good. He was horseback again, and it had been only when he climbed onto the back of the animal and ridden a little that it had come to him how much he had missed riding. There was something about the feel of a good horse beneath one, something about the way its muscles moved, about the way it lifted its feet, that gave to a man a sense of strength, a sense of well-being.

And this horse, he quickly learned, was an exceptionally fine animal. Not only was it careful about where it walked, but it seemed to understand that its rider was blind, and so it avoided low limbs as it threaded its way through the trees.

Hoka-hey, he shouted joyfully, shaking his lance in the air above his head,
this man gives thanks,
Grandfather,
that today is here, and that

he continues
to make
memories.

   In fact, as the old warrior thought of it, he really did feel good! The wounds from the wolves, if not healing as rapidly as he would have liked, were still healing nicely. This day his muscles and bones were giving him few problems, and on this horse he suddenly felt, for the first time since his vision had left him, that he could get along without his eyes.

   Dho, Man Above, he continued,
what of today?
Is this warrior to have
more trials? More troubles?
As he sits atop the
mountain
of his years
is he to make
more memories?
Must he do battle again?
No, this man does not
think so.
He has slain his brother
the bear,
and so has slain also
his fear.
He does not know what you,
Grandfather,
would have him do.
Yet he is ready,
and will do it
as he can.

   A little later the horse snorted and reared back a little, so the old man slid to the snow and discovered with his hands the trail of several other horses. For a few yards he crawled along feeling the depressions, and then he pulled himself back onto the horse and continued his journey.

There were either six or seven horses, all ridden, and the old man had the feeling it was a war party, though of course he could not tell from which nation they came. Yet as he rode he wondered, and the thought came again and again that they were Crows. He felt certain that the tracks had been made by the enemies of his people.

For most of the day the horse carried him forward through the silent drifts and across the bare ridges of a series of breaks that swept down and into the river bottoms. The silence was profound, and he could never remember feeling the stillness so deeply. It was as if all the earth had gone to sleep and would never awaken. For a time the old man almost felt that in all the world there was only himself and the buffalo runner, but when it suddenly snorted and wheeled around, he knew that such was not the case. Carefully he listened, straining his old ears, and then he heard the heavy panting that was now so familiar.

Dho, sheetshe, he mumbled.

The wolves were with him again!

Without hesitation he turned the horse and continued his journey, knowing that as long as they kept moving steadily the wolves would hold their distance. The old warrior did not fear them any longer, viewing them simply as brothers who were doing as their kind did to satisfy their hunger. Yet he was cautious, and he did his best to keep the horse calm while they kept a safe distance.

Late in the afternoon several deer bounded away from them down the hill, and as the old man listened he heard the wolves cry out and leave his trail in pursuit of new game. And it was shortly after that when the horse, of its own volition, suddenly turned from the trail of the Crows and climbed steadily up the crest of a wind-whipped ridge, its barren and rock-strewn surface totally unfriendly to any tracks at all.

Gradually yet steadily they climbed up through the pines and aspen until they emerged onto a flat tableland. This the horse carefully picked its way across, seeming as it did so to hide its own trail. The old man marveled and continued to let it have its head, feeling certain the horse was taking him where the Creator wanted him to go.

At dusk they came suddenly to an abrupt break, a canyon that was not visible until they were almost within it. The horse paused for a moment and then went over the edge, descending a steep game trail that entered almost immediately into a thick stand of fir and aspen.

For some time they moved steadily forward through the twilight, the old man sensing the movements of his horse carefully, noting with interest when it put its ears forward and snorted with excitement. Cautiously the aging warrior swung the horse around while he slid to the ground and once again examined it with his fingers. He then remounted and continued, and suddenly they broke into a small clearing where stood a lodge, a solitary lodge of his people.

Slowly he rode forward, still not sure exactly what he had found, but excited by the sudden aroma. Rapidly he felt over the area with his hands. The tepee was in bad shape and appeared to be empty, for he could smell only the stale odor of smoke long dead. Neither was there any recent sign of horses, nor were there any strips of meat hanging from the bare drying rack. Yet the snow near the doorflap was trampled, and the old man knew that someone was inside.

He cautiously moved forward, and it was when he reached for the opening that he first heard the singing, the soft low strength song sung by a woman as she prepared herself for death. Gently then the old man pulled aside the flap and stepped inside.

He knew instantly that he had been wrong about the fire. There was one, though it was very small, probably little more than coals. There were also some occupants in the lodge, yet it would be a few moments before he would learn that two women sat beyond the fire, three children huddled behind them, and beside them on the ground lay the still form of an adult warrior.

For an instant the two women stared at the old man in shocked disbelief, and then in terror they dropped the knives they had been holding in readiness and cowered back with the children, their wailing songs now become howlings of terror.

At first the old man did not understand why they should act in such a manner, but when one of the women wailed his name, he suddenly recognized the voice and understood what was wrong.

Standing as straight as his arthritic old bones would let him, in dignity befitting his position, he thought for a moment about what should be done. Out of respect, a man of the people never spoke directly to the wives of his sons, nor they to him. If communication were needed they spoke through others. That was the old way, and it was the good way. Still, these women were not the wives of his sons, but of his grandson, and he suddenly decided that he should converse directly with them

Dancing Moon, Little Feather,
do not fear.
This man is no spirit, but is still wearing
the same old wrinkled hide he
has always
worn.
It is true that he started on his journey to
the west,
but as you see,
he has been called back.
Now he is here, following many long hours
horseback.
Do you have something
to feed
an old man?

As he seated himself there was total silence within the lodge, and then Little Feather began wailing again, singing a song of shame and sorrow. In patience the old man listened, not understanding why these women should feel shame.

But then Dancing Moon spoke, telling him that they had no food at all, and they had had none for nearly three days. In a flood the story poured out, of how their husband, Smiling Wolf, had gone on a hunt and of how the boys had found him two days later, unconscious, with a Crow arrow through his chest. It had now been four days since they had dragged him home. He was still unconscious, and they had been without food for three long days. Nor dared they go far looking for any, for the Crows were still around, searching for the great warrior Smiling Wolf.

Silently the old man turned his back, hiding the tears of pity which he felt for these people, his family. Grasping his lance, he stood and shuffled out to his horse. There he removed the bear bladder full of pounded meat, offered a silent prayer of pity and sorrow, and then carried the meat back into the lodge. After seating himself once more, he handed the bladder to Dancing Moon. She took one look at it, smiled broadly, and began preparing a meal.

As they ate, the old man listened carefully to the activities of the two women and the three children. Dancing Moon seemed strong and eager. Little Feather, the larger of the two wives, sounded ill and seemed very weak. Of the children, only Happy Wind, the little girl, was sick, and she could hardly eat.

The two boys, Spotted Deer and Horse-That-Follows, were so frail and quiet that the old man could scarcely tell they were near. Spotted Deer, at eight summers, was the oldest. Horse-That-Follows, only six summers, was nearly as large as his brother and every whit his equal as far as believing in himself was concerned. In fact, he had earned his name because he was so strong, he followed Spotted Deer everywhere, and he would never admit that they were not equal in all they did. He was like a fine horse that would never stop going.

After the meal the old man broke the long silence.

Spotted Deer,
you and Horse-That-Follows saw me
coming
and came here to warn
the others.

It was more a statement than a question, and the boys, wide-eyed, nodded in agreement, forgetting he couldn't see them.

Hoka-hey! Yes you did!

You were hidden behind an aspen
which is bent as
an old man with many seasons upon
his shoulders.
Furthermore, as you turned to run,
one of you slipped,
yes, and narrowly missed going over
the cliff.

Now the boys were truly amazed, for they had told that to no one, no one at all. What was even more amazing, both of them knew that the old man was blind, going deaf, and mostly crippled. How, they wondered, could he have known?

And so the teaching began. The old man, as if reading their hearts, explained that by its actions his horse had shown him where they were. The slipping was there in the snow for all to see who cared to look. Even, he added with a grin, if they were blind and had to use their finger-eyes. Then the old man praised the lads, telling them that any men who could move that silently and that swiftly would one day be great warriors of the people.

At this both boys beamed with pride, and Horse-That-Follows forgot to feel foolish about slipping in the snow, something his older brother had contemptuously chastized him for.

Men!

Warriors!

Suddenly the boys had a new respect for this old man, this grandfather of their father, this wrinkled warrior who saw no light, who wore the white war-bonnet, who walked with three legs, and yet who had the strength and courage to praise two small boys for a deed well done.

The old man then examined Smiling Wolf, carefully applying his healing arts while he instructed the women about what they should do. The wound was very bad, and it had a foul smell to it, a sign that made the old man wonder that his grandson was alive at all.

Sensing that for the very first time he had won the confidence of the children, the old man turned back and gathered them about him, placing Happy Wind upon his lap. Then, in the warm and quiet darkness of the lodge he began talking, telling the children a story that he had learned when very young, a story designed to teach an important lesson.

When he finished he sat quietly, listening to the silence, wondering what the reactions of the children would be.

Finally Horse-That-Follows spoke, asking a question. The old man answered, another was asked, and suddenly he knew that the boys were seeing beyond his age and his ugliness, seeing into his years. They were ready to be taught.

Another story came to mind, that account brought forth another, and so he talked through his blindness of his own past when the days were bright and the nights short, teaching the children through his stories of lessons and values they so much needed to know. And as he talked, Dancing Moon fed ladles of warm broth into Little Feather, Happy Wind, and then into the unconscious form of Smiling Wolf.

Some of the stories the old man told were old, so very old that even his own grandfather, who had told them to him, could not tell when they were first told. Other stories he told were of things he himself had seen, of his own war parties, of the time he had killed the sacred white buffalo and had obtained its powers, and of course of the morning, just recently, when the Great Creator had given him the power to slay the giant bear.

This story fascinated the boys most of all, and even the women were silent as the old man dramatically related it detail by detail. When he had finished speaking, each in turn examined the pelt, exclaiming in awe at the long sharp claws and at the size of the giant head.

Long after the family was asleep, the old man stared into the comfortable darkness of his blindness. His thoughts seemed to ride with the wind that he knew swirled the smoke near the opening above the fire. His thoughts blew first to one thing and then to another, never following a straight pathway. He thought of old friends, of long-dead enemies, of his first real buffalo runner, of the lessons he had learned from his grandfather, and of that clear morning so long ago when he had gazed into the dawn and had suddenly, for the first time,

caught a glimpse of what life was about. In a flash he had understood that he was learning great lessons each day, both because of what he did and because of what others did. If those lessons remained with him alone, he realized, they would be of little value. Shared with others, however, the lessons he had learned would help to lighten their burdens, and would become of ever greater worth. All his life, therefore, he had done his best to share the thoughts of his heart and the experiences of his soul with those around him.

And now, when he had thought all that was past, he found himself teaching again, directing the lives of these people who suddenly had such a great need for him.

Ah, Grandfather, he spoke quietly into the darkness,
like the morning light
in the star nations,
perhaps this old man is at last,
beginning to glow.
Hoka-hey,
did you not see the eyes of those
little boys
dance
when this man spoke of his brother
the bear?
Even without sight this man could
see it.
And did you not see the glow of
their faces
when he called them
men,
when he called them
warriors?
And is it not so that we become
most quickly
the persons
we think we are?
  Ah, Grandfather,
as you have taught this creature,
so will he teach these children,

by convincing them that they are,
in fact,
the people you and he know
they must, one day,
become.

And so the days passed quickly as the old man sat in the
warmth of the lodge of his grandson, teaching the ways of a
true man to the children. Each day when the weather permit-
ted he would either have the boys lead him along the paths
near their lodge, or he would sit in front, nodding approval of
the little woman-things Happy Wind was learning or of the
man-feats of the two boys. In truth, the children became his
eyes, his ears and his feet, and never were two young boys
and a little girl so anxious to please. Constantly they would
run to him with news of the childish things that so delighted
their fancy, and he was always as happy as he could be to hear
of them. The two women wondered that an old man should
get so excited over the things of children, but one day Dancing
Moon suddenly found understanding, and quietly she explained to her sister-wife that it was the children the old man
was excited about, not their childish things. He was making
the children *feel* important, that one day they would *be* important. That was the way of a teacher, of a true man.

Many other things did the two wives discuss about the
grandfather of their husband. Now that he had returned, they
both found themselves wondering a great deal about him. As
Dancing Moon expressed it, the old man who was now directing their lodge had changed. He was not the same ancient
warrior whom their husband had placed upon the scaffold.
Neither of the women could decide exactly how he was different, how he had changed, unless it was that he seemed
stronger, more sure of himself, more certain about what he
was doing.

And Dancing Moon also noticed another change, a change
that came from within herself. Prior to the old man's supposed
death, she had only tolerated him, literally forcing herself to
lead him around and care for him. She wasn't certain why he
repulsed her so, whether it was his blindness and helpless-

ness, his death-like appearance, his quavering voice that
moaned out of his toothless mouth, the odor of age that was
about him, or simply the fact that he was so far removed from
her in age, so far removed from the things she knew and the
experiences she felt and enjoyed.

But now all those feelings had fled her heart, and with
surprise she found herself being drawn closer and closer to
him. Certainly he was still blind and needed much help.
Obviously he still looked and acted old, older even than she
could imagine. Yet now she understood that despite his age
and attendant problems he was still a man. In fact, he was a
man who was very similar to her stricken husband. And as she
thought of him in that way he became much easier to understand. His thoughts, his feelings, and even his actions were no
different from those of a young man, except perhaps that they
were restricted by age. And as she thought of this, Dancing
Moon suddenly understood that the grandfather of her husband was not so far removed from her own feelings and
experiences as she had thought. In fact, he probably understood more about her and the thoughts and feelings of her
heart than she did about herself. And he did so because he had
had longer, much longer, to feel and to think about and to
understand the emotions she was just now learning to feel.
Now she recalled the words she had heard him speak to her
husband one evening, words that had made little sense to her
at the time.

My son,
a man will never learn
all he needs to know
with just one
experience.
Experiences must pile up,
as boulders do
at the foot of the cliff
of a man's life.
And as they pile up,
each one will give him
insight

into the others,
giving him the time
he needs
to evaluate and to think
about them.
In that way only
will a man learn
the lessons
Wanken tanka
would have him learn
from the experiences
he chooses to give
him.

And now Dancing Moon understood that age, while usually handicapping an individual physically, actually gave him greater freedom and greater wisdom spiritually and mentally. It was this wisdom, this freedom, that was so visible in the old man, that was drawing her to him so strongly. No wonder he was having such an impact upon her and upon the children. No wonder she found such delight in watching and feeling the interaction between her family and their ancestor. What a special thing it was to have him with them!

One day, on one of his walks with the boys, the old man paused to rest against a large cottonwood near their lodge. He couldn't get over the feeling of having to rely so completely upon these children and the women. Yet as he thought of it he suddenly realized that the boys were becoming much more responsible, more able to lead him than they had been. And then a thought came to him, a new thought, a thought that would not leave him alone.

Grandfather,
this old warrior
just thought of a new thing,
and he would
question it.
Do all things
happen

for good?
Is it good for a man
to suffer
pain, misery and
loneliness
most of
the days of his life?
    Dho, this old man
thinks maybe so.
Could it be that
all things are
good,
if not for the one who
suffers,
then at least for others who
would learn
from his suffering?
    In this man's
multitude of
years
there is much weakness,
much helplessness, and
much sorrow.
He does not enjoy this
at all.
Yet from it these
little ones
and the women
seem to be learning.
This old warrior feels,
suddenly,
that he has been selfish,
that he has not been
willing
to share
what he is
with them,
simply because he has not

enjoyed it
himself.
O Great Creator,
give this man
courage
to live this lesson you
have just
shown him.

After a moment he called the boys to him, thanked them for leading him so carefully and so well, and then asked them to examine the tree against which he had been leaning. When they had looked carefully he asked Spotted Deer to describe the tree to him, all of it. When he was finished the old man spoke again.

My sons,
the branches of a tree in winter
are like the paths this old man has trod
in life.
They go in all directions.
Some are sturdy and have led
to much happiness.
Others, too fragile to stand, have led
to many sorrows.
Yes, this tree reaching upward to the sky,
with its bare branches tangled, is like
the paths of life.
They seemed confusing when they were taken,
for the leaves of this man's
summer
kept him from seeing clearly.
Yet now, in the bareness of his
winter,
He sees that each path,
like each branch,
had a purpose, to strengthen the roots
of his life, to help him become the man

he has become,
to help him become the man
he is to be.

  That night he stood alone outside the lodge, and once more, as had happened so many times in the past, he was struck with the beauty of the night. Even though he could no longer see, he could remember well the sights of the evening, and as his ears picked up the sounds, his mind brought them clearly to his vision. Out in the darkness an owl hooted as it drifted down the corridors between the pines, and above him the man knew the stars glowed closely like multitudes of camp-fires spread out across the star nations.

  O Grandfather,
how old memories seem to flood
by,
tumbling forward out of the past like a
churning, foaming stream when the snow
has begun to melt.
It is good that the joy
of remembering
is as strong as the pain,
for that comes without warning,
slicing deeply into
one's heart.
  Walking back from here along
the pathways of the mind,
all that this man sees of his
life
are the great round rocks,
and not their jagged edges,
nor the small and unimportant
stones.
These have been ground to nothing and
washed away
by the river of time,
leaving him with nothing to remember
but good things.

He knows that he has experienced
pain,
yet the scars have healed and are now
hidden in his
wrinkles,
much as the bark of a tree
hides its old wounds.
Where this man walked there seemed to be much of
sadness,
yet he remembers now mostly the good things —
the touch of his woman, Tashina,
the joy of victory,
the pride of riding into battle
beside a tall son.
He knows there was much on the earth to make him
unhappy,
but somehow there was never
time
to listen to the broken song
others seemed determined to sing.
There was always too much joy in
the mornings,
too much beauty in
the afternoons,
and too much softness in
the darkness.
*   Grandfather,*
one finds it a good thought
that he has been able to sing
a whole song
during his life.
Now his memories are mostly of
happy things, the things that have all come together
at last,
to make this, your creation, the man that
he is.
*   One of the little ones, Horse-That-Follows,*
asked today
if this man was lonely.

He said no, because he is not,
not in the way the boy was thinking.
But you know, O Great One,
that this man is lonely, lonely for his friends
who were
and who have now taken that long journey
to the west.
And of course, he is lonely for one
special person,
his Tashina,
most of all.
But the pain of that sweet memory
is great,
and so he does not allow himself to think often
of her.
Still, some days her memory comes despite his efforts,
and it is almost like she is with him
once more.
His happiness then is great, but so is the
pain when she must leave. It is for
that reason only that he tries not to
remember her.
   There is one thing more,
Grandfather.
For many seasons
this man has longed for the way
things were
when others depended upon him.
He missed being in the center
of life,
for it is lonely on
its edge.
Now he sees that he
need never
have been on the edge
at all,
for always others have
needed him.
Just not in

the same
way.

And so the days passed and the children learned quickly
under the direction of the old man. He gave them as much
responsibility as he was able, teaching them through their
own decisions as well as his own. As he expected, they frequently made mistakes, some of them quite serious. Once,
when the meat from the bear was gone and their tiny brothers
the rabbits were no longer seeking their snares and lures, the
old man directed the boys to a place where he was certain they
could find deer. They had only their small bows, but he felt
that they might get close enough to bring one down. They did
find deer, but for three days they were too anxious and care-
less, and their noise frightened the animals.

It became a time of hunger for them all, yet the old man told
Dancing Moon to let no one complain. Then, each night when
the boys returned empty-handed and more sorrowful and
upset than the night before, he would gather them around the
fire and tell them happy stories, lesson stories that would
teach as well as stories told simply for fun. All would laugh
until they could laugh no more, and the lesson ultimately
learned was that when there was nothing else, a belly full of
laughter made the long nights go much more quickly.

On the third night, the old man lay for hours staring into the
darkness of his life, his own empty stomach growling and
twisting itself into knots around his spine. Despite their hunger they had had an especially joyful evening. The children
had laughed harder than he had ever heard them laugh when
he had, with mock-serious reverence, gathered up one of each
pair of their moccasins and handed them to Dancing Moon,
telling her to make a delicious stew of them. Even he had
laughed at her clowning antics as she pretended to prepare the
stew.

Ah, Grandfather, he at last spoke,
it seems to me that this man laughed more
when he was younger.
And it feels very good

to laugh again.
Was the earth happier when he was young?
He does not think so.
The sun woke each morning and
trailed all day to the west,
as it does today.
People were born and
people died,
and there was hunger and plenty then,
as now.
No, the earth has not changed so much,
nor the people.
It must be that
this old man has.
Do you know, Grandfather,
that as this man considers this,
the things that bother him now
gave him much laughter
when he was
young.
Sheetshe! That is bad!
Happy things
should never stop
bringing laughter.

On their fourth day of hunger young Spotted Deer loosed an arrow that found its mark. The old man had never known two boys more excited or filled with well-earned pride as they led the horse into camp dragging a small doe behind.

Hoka-hey, Grandfather, he said as he heard them approach, turning his face toward the sky,
were there ever two warriors
more mighty?
Were there ever two who deserved more
to be called
men?

Later, when all had eaten their fill of roast venison, the old man spoke again.

My sons,
today you did a great thing, for you
killed the deer and
fed the hunger of
us all.
And little Happy Wind,
my daughter,
you too did well,
for you helped your mother remove the skin and
prepare the meal which
fed us.
Do not forget,.
little warriors,
to thank the Great Creator
for allowing the deer its
birth
so that this day we might eat.
Touch the earth now,
each of you,
and do not forget that as the deer has gone to it,
so too one day must we follow.
The earth sings the same song today
that it sang for our fathers
when their laughter
warmed the day,
when their tears
filled up the
night.
Maka, the earth, sings a song
of hope.
Maka sings a song
of joy.
Maka rises up and laughs
at us
each time we forget how spring begins
with winter,
and how death begins
with birth.
That is a good thought, and
a happy thought also,

for we know always where
the path
of our life will one day
lead.

It was Horse-That-Follows, the next day, who saw the Crow warrior up on the tableland, and it was that day also that the wolves arrived.

The old man, having sent the boys for another deer, was dozing in the afternoon sun, now and then awakening to think of days gone by and of the people who had gone with them. Spotted Deer had hidden himself along a game trail, and Horse-That-Follows had carefully circled above in the hope that he might drive a deer down to where his brother was hiding. But he had gone a little higher than he planned, suddenly finding himself on the rim above the canyon. Almost instantly he had seen the Crow warrior, who appeared to be working his way toward the canyon, trying to follow some dim trail.

Cautiously the boy slid off the rim, then he ran swiftly to where Spotted Deer was hidden. After a quick conference, the two fled down the hill to their lodge, where they reported what Horse-That-Follows had seen.

For a long time the old man sat unmoving, his eyes closed, and the boys, impatient, wondered if he had heard them. At last he spoke, telling them that they had done well. Then he requested only that they tether the horse to some aspen near where the old man sat.

The boys, unable to understand, did as they were told with a great deal of impatience. When they had finished they found him sitting as before, his eyes tightly closed. For a moment or two they waited, but finally Horse-That-Follows could stand it no longer, and he spoke to the old man.

Grandfather, do you not wish that I go to the rim and watch for our enemies the Crows? I could then run back with word of them.

No, my little son.
That is not necessary.

There is only one man now, and our buffalo runner
will tell us of
his approach.
No, we need not
fear him alone.
But in one day,
perhaps two,
he will bring others.
Those we must prepare for.

   But how, Grandfather? asked Spotted Deer. *How can we who*
are so few and so small fight against a war party of Crows? And why
are they here? What do they seek us for?

·

Ah, so many questions,
my son.
But questions show a desire
to learn,
and that is good.
The Crows seek us because they fear
your father.
They do not know that he lies
halfway along the road
to the west.
They know only that in
terrible battle
he was wounded, and now they seek to
destroy him before
he can return the battle
to them.
That is their way.
Our way must be to defend your father,
he and the women.
It is true that we are not many.
It is true that we are not large.
But this old man has seen your hearts,
little warriors,
and there are none larger
or more brave

among all the people.
With your hearts full of
courage
we will fight,
and the Great Creator
will decide the
victor.

Carefully then the old man questioned the boys about the terrain which surrounded them, mapping in his mind, as they spoke, a plan of defense against the Crows. Every possibility was considered carefully, and then under his direction the boys and the women prepared for the battle which the old man felt certain was coming.

Longingly he gazed with his sightless eyes in the direction of his unconscious grandson. Oh, for his strength, his courage, his skill in battle. Oh, that he would arise and be well again. Gladly would the old man have traded places with him. But such thinking was folly, he knew, and so was time wasted. He must think only of the Crows, and of how he and the children might stop them. His thinking, that and the courage of two boys, a girl and two women, was certainly not much with which to stop a war party of Crows.

It was long after dark when all the preparations had been completed and tried out, and it was a very tired group who gathered around the fire to eat. Carefully the old man felt the faces of these people, his people. There was much good within them, and he felt a sense of pride that the children, and in a sense the women, sprang from his loins.

Yet in their faces he could also feel fear, a fear that he knew might cripple more than a wound. He thought then of the wolves, his vision, and of the death of his brother the great bear, and with that thought in mind he began to speak.

When this man was young he knew
very little.
Although he was big and thought himself
a man, he had never
grown

in the way a true man
must grow.
So one day he vowed
a dance
to the sun.
That is the way of our people,
and we do it
that we might gain strength
and bring good
upon us.
The pain was worse than a man
can say,
and his mouth opened
to cry out,
but the wind came and
blew
the sound away.

Each day for three days
his eyes followed the tracks of
the sun
as it trailed across
the sky,
seeing but not seeing,
and finally the sun
blinded
his ignorance.
Each day his hands
grasped
the sacred sage and the
sacred rattle,
but they had never learned to truly
feel,
and so at last they died.
Each day his ears
listened
to the music of the
sacred drums,
but they had never learned to truly
hear,

and so at last they were
drowned
in a roaring sound.
All this continued until this man was reduced to
nothing.
And then the Creator awakened him.
Speak the truth, said Wanken tanka.
The wind blew back his voice and
the man admitted
he was afraid.
See the reason, said the Creator.
The sun gave him back his vision and
he saw all things changing,
including himself.
Feel truly sacred things, said the Great One.
His hands came to life and he held
his children
in his arms.
Hear true music, said the Creator.
The roaring left his ears
and he heard
his people
laughing.
Do you know what you are? asked
Wanken tanka,
and he said,
At last I am a man.
*   My sons,*
change is a part of being
a man,
but most men resist it,
and fear.
Yet when we hear, see
and feel
true things,
as a man should,
then great courage comes from the Creator,
which puts all fear
behind.

Then is a man truly happy.
This is what this old man has learned.

Quietly tiny flames licked up the sides of the logs in the small fire, their flickering tongues casting dancing images of the occupants of the tepee on its buffalo-hide walls. Outside the wind picked up, and a few flakes from a new snowstorm drifted through the smoke opening.

It was at that moment that a wolf raised its spine-tingling cry out in the timber. A little later another lifted its lonely voice from a different direction, and the old man knew that his hungry brothers were back again.

Softly he directed that the horse be brought within the lodge, and then they were all silent once more, thinking their thoughts as they listened to the sounds of the wolves and of the growing storm. At last they slept, and while they did the snow fell, and the rising wind whipped it into long drifts. Slowly their tracks, and even the landmarks, disappeared, and the world became changed. The wind howled and those lesser killers, the savage timber wolves, burrowed deep under the boughs of an old pine and hid to wait out the storm, one with belly half-filled, one nearly starving. But there would be nothing for either of them to eat until the storm was over, and they knew it. For during the storm nothing moved, nothing but the wind — the wind, the snow, and the Crows.

Part Five

The Battle

With daylight came the Crows, not noisily and with war-whoops, but stealthily, as if they were trying to remain in harmony with the silent, snow-filled canyon. The occupants of the lodge were certain of their nearness only when the horse suddenly lifted its head and stared at the wall of the tepee, its attitude one of rapt attention.

Earlier, long before the light from the new day had begun to color the sky, the family had been awake. From small comments the old man knew that Spotted Deer was terrified, perhaps even more than the others. Gently he placed a wrinkled hand on the boy's shoulder and squeezed, softly reminding him of the love and strength they had found within their family. He also reminded him of the knowledge they had that the Great Creator, Wanken tanka, was over all and would see that all things worked out for their good.

Now, my family, he continued,
today we will indeed
fight the Crows.

This man has lived long enough to learn that
fighting
is not always a good way.
But he has also lived long enough
to understand
that a man must protect the family
the Great Wanken tanka has
given him.

But Grandfather, Spotted Deer interrupted, *if we were to go*
unarmed to them and explain that our father is far along the road to
the west and that there are no other warriors among us—

My son, the old man spoke quietly,
this man is happy that you
desire peace, for that is
the way of
a true man.
Yet you should understand that
hunters such as these like nothing
better
than to see
the hunted
come walking to them
unarmed.
One cannot submit
to evil
without encouraging evil
to grow.
Each time a man gives up
a principle,
each time he allows
evil
to destroy what he knows
is right
or good,
he is saying to evil,
This man supports you.

Sadly, greed and thirst for
power
are never
satisfied.
There is always hunger for more.
Hopefully there may come
a time
when men of
all nations
will lose this hunger and
this thirst.
Perhaps then they will be
more willing to
listen
and to trust
one another.
But there will never come
a time
when a man should compromise
himself
or his beliefs
endeavoring to gain such trust.
That is what evil
would desire.
And such compromise is wrong.
Always!
That is why a
true warrior
will rise above his fear
and do battle.
That is why
this day
we must fight.

   Now, they are many, while
we are few. And so we know that
the battle
will not be easy.
Perhaps the Crows will

overpower us,
and if that is to be so, today
will be a very good day
to die.
Do you understand?
   Do you understand that
today every living thing is in agreement
with us?
Today our memories are of
happy things.
Today we think evil of
no one.
Today the earth shines in
our eyes.
Today we know we defend
the right.
Today we feel no pain,
only happiness.
Today our lodge is filled
with laughter.
Most important, however,
today we are surrounded by
our family,
our courageous family.
Today would indeed be a good day
to die.

   Timidly then, little Spotted Deer looked up at the old man
and asked if he didn't fear death, even a little.

   Ah, my son, he replied after a moment's thought,
death is a thing
that is always with
a man,
from the hour of his birth
until after he draws
his final
breath.
Only then does death cease

to be a part
of life.
To a youth death seems
an enemy,
one to be feared.
But as the days of
his life
flee past,
he learns that enemies are,
in reality,
friends,
for they teach him great lessons
about himself,
lessons that must be learned.
So too with death.
    In the winter of a man's life
the lonely wind of death
drifts quietly down
out of the darkening
sky,
bearing on its
icy breath
the snowy remnants
of autumn's last
rain.
And with a quiet sighing
it tugs
at his hair,
gently
encouraging him,
lifting him
to his tottering
feet.
Then for just
a moment
he hears,
once more,
the singing of the wind
in the trees,

and feels the wonder of
new snow held in childish
hands.
Before him he sees,
as he
has daily for
years,
the face of his
woman, smiling
the same way she smiled
on their first night
together.
It has been good,
this life.
But like the
wind
and his woman
it has flown by,
leaving him old and lonely,
wrinkled and
cold,
with nowhere to go, nowhere
but onward,
*   It is then,*
my son,
that death becomes a
welcome guest,
welcome at last because
a man finally sees
that death is not
the end,
but is instead, simply
a continuing step in
his life.

Smiling then, the old man added a final thought.

Yet, my children,
this old man does not think that today

is the day
when death will come, at least
for us.

Softly then he called the two women to him. To Little
Feather he handed Happy Wind, the tiny girl who had
cuddled on his lap so often since his return. To Dancing
Moon, the smallest and yet the strongest of heart, he gave
merely his smile and a soft pat on the arm. Somehow he knew
how she would respond this day.

Next he placed his hands upon the two boys, fiercely
painted as much to give them courage as to frighten the
Crows. Oh, if only their father could see them! He then reminded them of where they were to be and of what they were
to do, and each boy spoke gravely and with understanding.

Finally he offered a prayer of gratitude and supplication,
and then he sent the boys out into the dawning, toward their
destiny.

And what a day that was! Yes, and what stories would be
made that day! In long years to come, multitudes of the people
would sit around their fires at night and speak of the battle
fought by the sightless old man as he sat within his lodge,
gaining victory over his enemies through the eyes of two small
boys and a courageous warrior-woman.

Laughter would ring as the storyteller spoke of the snares
and of the ice slide that the boys, under the old man's direction, had built. The slide led to the cliff edge, and down its
steep and slippery surface several of the Crows made an
unexpected departure when they were led onto it by a small,
apparently fleeing, warrior.

Sorrow would appear as the listeners would hear how the
old man was wounded, and pride would show as the speaker
told of tiny arrows that flew true, of the desperate footrace that
was won by a warrior of only six summers, and of the warrior-
woman who all alone sent a man of the Crow along his road to
the west, wounded another, and then in a showing of true
courage cared for his and the old man's wounds.

Looks of awe would encompass their faces as the listeners
heard of the Crow who dived beneath the boughs of a large

pine to make an ambush, only to find that he was sharing space with two near-starved timber wolves. What a noise there must have been as all three boiled out of the snow, flew over the ridge and right onto the icy slide (almost as if it had been planned) where they quickly disappeared.

And finally, laughter would peal out once more as the teller would relate how the two boy-warriors and their warrior mother, knowing that nothing could be done, simply turned their backs upon the tumultuous noise leaping up from beneath the cliff, leaving Crows and wolves to work things out below as best they were able.

Ah, what a day that was, and what stories were made that day! It was indeed a good day, but as the old man had said, it was not a good day for dying.

Part Six

The Windwalker

As Dancing Moon and her two strong sons returned to the lodge after the battle, they found Little Feather howling in fear and grief as she roughly cleaned the wound on the old man's head, periodically shouting insults at the unconscious Crow warrior whom Dancing Moon had rendered helpless. Dancing Moon slid from the horse and gently pushed the larger woman aside, telling her to care for Happy Wind. She then began to minister to the old man, softly explaining to her sister-wife that old people needed as much gentleness as did children.

Meanwhile the two boys started to drag out the unconscious form of the Crow, known as Two Strikes, intending to push him over the slide with the others. But at that the old man raised his head up and with a lifted hand stopped them. He then directed a very unwilling Dancing Moon to care for the wounds she had so recently inflicted upon her enemy, and the two boys and Little Feather stared in open-mouthed amazement as she angrily did so. The old man then taught them another lesson story, a story of Tashina and her Crow killers, and of courage, true courage, that shows itself through compassion. By the time he was finished, Dancing Moon was being as gentle with the Crow called Two Strikes as she had been earlier with the old man.

All the other Crows had vanished, and Spotted Deer later found the trail of two horses going up over the rim of the canyon. He also found five Crow horses standing where their owners had left them, and so the family became wealthy with horses, the most valuable commodity of the people.

Thus the winter passed quickly, and it was in the moon of new buds that Smiling Wolf got up and walked into the world of spirits. He did so gently and quietly, and so the grief of his family at his passing was also gentle and quiet. Truly they were lonely for him, but he had been long asleep and, as the old man said, he would now awaken in the beautiful land to the west, and there he would wait for them, happy as only one in that land could be.

Besides, he gently explained, looking with strong affection upon the two boys who now sat straight as warriors and at the little girl who sat so proudly beside her mother, Smiling Wolf could now go in peace, knowing that he left behind to care for his lodge two warriors that all the people could be proud of, and one little daughter who would be taught true woman-hood by her mother.

The day after Smiling Wolf was placed upon the scaffold, Little Feather disappeared. One of the horses was gone also, but no one said anything, for all understood that with no children of her own to tie her to the family, she would wish to wander and to mourn alone.

Many weeks later, when Old Man Winter had released his hold, Two Strikes, the Crow warrior, suddenly appeared, carrying across the withers of his horse a fat buck. Under the careful eye of Dancing Moon he had recovered quickly, and one morning when there was still much snow on the ground he was gone. He took no horse and left no trail, and Dancing Moon found herself wondering many things and thinking many thoughts about this man who had once been her enemy.

And now he was back, bringing a gift of meat. He said

nothing, merely dropping the deer to the ground, looking for a long moment at Dancing Moon, and then wheeling his horse to vanish quickly into the forest.

The old man, listening intently to all that transpired, suddenly grinned a sly grin and began singing a happy song, an old and timeless song of love. Dancing Moon, turning to look at the old man, was instantly aware that he was seeing through his blindness and into her heart. In complete confusion and embarrassment she fled into the lodge, leaving little Happy Wind to try to dress the deer alone, and her sons to wonder at what was going on.

Ah, Grandfather, the old man said that night as he stood alone beneath the fragrant and whispering pines,
Dancing Moon is a good woman,
very good for
the children.
And the way she moves around
the fire,
well,
she moves a great deal like Tashina,
though this old man has not noticed that
until recently.
And now he knows of the shining in
her eyes,
the glow that means she is ready
to find happiness
again.
This man too longs for happiness,
Grandfather,
and if he remains here, then
neither Dancing Moon nor he
will find it.
Dancing Moon will not find it because
she is too much a true
woman,
because she respects the grandfather
of her husband,
and will not bring another man into

her lodge
while he is there.
And this man you, of course, understand.
Each day he grows more
lonely,
each day he feels the
earth
to find it a little
harder.
Each day the sights and sounds
of his life grow
more dim,
each day his old heart aches
a little more for
Tashina.
Ah, Grandfather,
is it not yet time?

That night was one of the hardest the old man could ever recall spending. Every bone, muscle and sinew seemed to ache separately, and by morning he was exhausted and ill. Yet even then there was no relief, for the agony was as bad sitting in the sunlight, his bent old back supported against the lodge, as it was when he was lying down. No matter which way he moved or positioned himself, he still suffered pain.

Yet the day was beautiful, and several times the old man thought he heard the clear notes of his sister the lark, though how he could with his ears as they were he wasn't certain.

Late that afternoon, with little Happy Wind sitting upon his lap tickling his chin, the old man was suddenly aware of a new thought, a thought in his mind that seemed to say over and over, here is why.

Here is why!

Each man learns love as he gives of himself to others, and this gift he gives to them, they too must one day share, thus learning love themselves. That was the truth of the sacred hoop or circle, taught him by the red eagle of his vision, Wanken tanka, and it is the ultimate purpose of life. It is all for love!

And as that thought darted back and forth across the pathways of his mind, a smile creased his wrinkled face, a smile so wide that for a time even his pains vanished.

Following their evening meal little Happy Wind took her place again on his lap, and the old man told them a happy story, a story of the coyote and the bright star of the star nations which glows with happiness just at dusk.

When he was through and all were laughing in merriment, he suddenly found himself doubled over with a knot of pain in his belly that was bigger than anything he had ever encountered. For long and agonizing moments he endured in silence, patiently bearing the humility of having his family see him rendered thus. At length, when he was able, he sat erect and spoke again.

Now, my children, this man feels
that the time has come
to tell you another
story,
a story about dying.
It too is a happy story, and
should not make you
sad.
Many seasons ago, when winter was coming,
this man found himself alone
one day
in the forest,
It was a beautiful day,
and his soul sang as he
beheld
the brilliant color the sun gave
the leaves of the maples, a color
more beautiful than a man can ever describe.
As he drank from the stream, he saw
that it danced
slowly over
the rocks,
making a song of
ending.

The creatures too, the four-footers
and the wings of the air,
were themselves singing a
slow song,
telling this man
that they too understood the
song
of ending.
Many of them were dancing
their last dance,
and the quiet music of the stream and
the gentle voice of the wind
made beautiful music
while they prepared
for death.
*   Yet there was no fear nor sadness,*
not in the golden leaves,
not in the stream
nor among the creatures
who were preparing for
Old Man Winter,
for all was as it should be,
and had been,
and would be,
always.
You see, winter is the season of
death,
and nature does not fight against it.
She simply prepares for it.
Thus, when it comes time to die,
there is happiness,
for all creatures understand
that death is not
the end. They know that
the sacred circle of new life begins with
the death
of the old one.
*   Do you see?*
Old leaves fall and nourish the ground that

new leaves might spring forth
in strength.
Creatures too nourish the earth
as they die,
their spirits drifting away to
the west
on the night
wind.
And old men die that
young men might take their places,
learning the joys that old men
have known.
Thus there is happiness
everywhere,
here, and in the world
of spirits.
   And so as this man moved through the forest,
he saw that there was much getting ready,
much rejoicing,
and much in the way of the last dance.
   Much later, when the season of cold
had passed,
this man walked once more
through
the forest.
The leaves on the maple trees were
fresh
and green,
and the creatures—the
four-footers and the
wings
of the air—
were all dancing,
dancing the mating dance.
The wind was quick
and fresh,
the stream was swift
and pure,
and the songs they made

as they danced through
the leaves
and over the
rocks
were songs of
beginning.
This song is a happy song that
each of us may
learn,
and then sing once or twice before
it is time to teach it to
our children.
    My strong sons,
my beautiful daughters,
this old man who sits before you
has sung the song of
beginning life.
He has danced with Tashina the
mating dance,
and children and children's children
and their children
have walked
the earth.
And now in his winter
the sun
has warmed him once more, and
the Great Wanken tanka has allowed him
to dance again
with happiness,
as he has watched his sons become
men,
as he has watched his daughters become
women.
    But now the sun has fallen into
the earth,
and his last dance
is finished.
It is now his turn
to nourish the

earth
while his spirit
walks on the
wind
into the land of
the west,
where those who have gone
before
await him.
This he does that your own songs may be
sung.
This he does that your own dances may be
danced.
    Little warriors,
Little mother,
Dancing Moon,
take hold and cling to only good things,
for good things will always
bring happiness.
Cling to the earth
for she is our mother.
Cling to what you know
is true,
even if you are like the tree
in the meadow,
all alone.
Cling to compassion,
even when the one you care for
has been,
or will yet be,
your enemy.
Cling to what you must do,
no matter how difficult
the task
becomes.
Cling to life,
for in each new day
the Great Wanken tanka
has hidden a little happiness.
We have but to find it, and then

it is ours forever.
Finally, cling to this wrinkled old hand
even when it has gone away
from you.
Cling tightly to all of these things,
and you will be
the men
you wish to be,
the women
you wish to be.

Happy Wind gently squeezed the old man's neck while a tear from her eyes rolled down his wrinkled cheek. Slowly then the boys walked past him, holding his hand for a moment in manly dignity before they retired. At last Dancing Moon, with tears in her eyes, walked up to the old man. Carefully he took her hand and gently he squeezed it, telling her better in that way than he could in any other that he loved her and was pleased with her new happiness.

Through that night his pain was worse even than it had been the night before, and so, long after the others slept, he rose quietly to his feet, wrapped the bearskin about himself, took one long look with his sightless old eyes at those he loved so dearly, and then shuffled out of the lodge.

At once his horse was there, the buffalo runner that had come to him so mysteriously. Together they walked to a low hummock, and from that the old man was able to climb to the horse's back. Quietly then he rode out of the clearing, not seeing at all the tear-stained faces that watched his leaving. Up through the aspen he rode, the aspen with their white spectral trunks glowing softly in the darkness. And then he rode through the soft blackness of the fragrant pine and fir, always upward, always higher.

At last he emerged from the canyon, and on the top of a high hill the horse paused, giving the old man a chance to feel the night.

Grandfather,
this old creation of yours
loves the darkness.

Even the darkness
of no sight
is beautiful.
The air is cold and clear,
and a moment ago, or
so it seems,
he smelled the woodsmoke from where
his family sleeps
around the fire.
How is it that
with all else gone,
he is still able to smell?
For little things like that this tired old man
gives thanks.
Now he is here,
alone in his blindness.
Once he would have worried
that thought,
like a dog worrying a bone,
till it left him filled
with sadness.
But now, Grandfather,
such thoughts no longer affect him.
He is unmoved.
Everything has passed beyond him
and there are no new losses left
to fear.
No, not even death.
So many things that once seemed
important
no longer have significance.
Acquiring horses,
seeking fame,
knowing victory—
somehow it is too late
to worry about
all that.
Somehow it is too late
to—

Ah, Grandfather,
what a fine joke
this has been,
saving such a good portion of
this man's life
until he thought his life
was past.
Thank you for allowing him to be
a teacher,
to be a part of his
family
once more.
Thank you for allowing him to meet his brother
the bear
once more.
And, Hoka-hey,
wasn't that a fine battle
the little ones
fought?
Grandfather, did you see the way
our children put
those Crows to
rout?
And Dancing Moon,
did you see how—

And the old man broke into a happy chuckle, thinking not only of the way she fought but of the way she cared for the wounded man who had been her enemy and who had now returned.

Most of all, Grandfather,
thank you for allowing this old man,
this old fool,
to see
with the eyes of his feelings
the life,
the love,
the happiness

in their eyes.
That is a memory he
will cherish
always.
   But now what,
O Great One?
This man aches with longing for Tashina.
Still, he will do as you—

At that moment a strong warm wind drifted up out of the canyon, a wind that caught at the bearskin and at the white hair that Dancing Moon had so carefully braided for the old man. The horse stirred, and the warrior felt stabs of pain as his old bones groaned anew, pain that he was certain would never end.

But then quickly it did, and he wondered at the ease with which he turned upon the horse's back to see the dawn. For it was dawn, suddenly, and now he wondered how it had grown light so quickly, without his noticing that it was coming.

The dawn! The old man could see the—

Again the wind gusted out of the canyon, and as it did so the old man heard his name, from far off in the west someone was calling his name. Straining his eyes against the glare, he struggled to see who it was who knew his youth name and who called him. And then he did see, coming down the side of a beautiful green hill, and his heart leaped within him.

Crooked Horse!

Crooked Horse, the friend of his youth! He who was killed by the bear! It was him, it was—

And then suddenly the old man knew that he had but to step out. Hesitantly he did so, first one step and then another. Then, with excitement mounting, he ran three or four steps. And he did it easily, without pain. Suddenly he threw back his head and laughed, laughed with joy and happiness so pure that it amazed even himself.

But then he stopped, staring in wonder. For behind Crooked Horse stood his son Little Bear and his grandson Smiling Wolf, standing with their arms folded awaiting him. Quickly he moved toward them, wishing to tell them of their children, of the little ones who had learned so well. But somehow they already seemed to know, to understand, and as he reached them they turned, smiling, and he was forced to stop again, once more filled with amazement. For before him stood Tashina, somehow changed and yet still beautiful, more beautiful even than he remembered her.

Hesitantly he moved toward her, fearing that she would vanish as she had done so many times before. But she didn't and then they were together and were holding each other and she was real and they were laughing and they were walking off together and the wind was blowing gently behind them, behind them and around them and beneath them, carrying them westward, westward toward the green, green hills.

And only a little distance away the horse nickered once and then moved off the hill, its empty burden already slipping from its back to return to the earth. The old man was, at last, the Windwalker.